On the Color Case

Dalmatian Press, 2007. All rights reserved. Printed in the U.S.A. 1-866-418-2572
The DALMATIAN PRESS name, logo, and Tear and Share are trademarks of Dalmatian Publishing Group, LLC, Franklin, Tennessee 37067.
No part of this book may be reproduced or copied in any form without written permission from the copyright owner.

07 08 09 10   NGS 10 9 8 7 6 5 4 3 2
16336 Disney My Friends Tigger and Pooh 8x8 - On the Color Case!

One day in the Hundred-Acre Wood, Pooh, Piglet, and Rabbit were painting the backdrop for their new play: *The Busy Buzzy Bees*.

"A bright blue sky," said Rabbit.

"A pretty red flower," said Piglet.

"A friendly yellow bee," said Pooh, "who will visit the red flower, then fly through the blue sky to the big honey tree."

"Hmmmm…" pondered Pooh. "Honey trees make me think of honey.
And that makes my tummy rumbly. Piglet and Rabbit, do you suppose
it might be that time of day when a snack would be nice?"

"Indeed!" agreed Rabbit.
"Yes, yes, yes!" said Piglet.
"That is just what I was supposing," said Pooh.

So the three painters left the
scene to enjoy an afternoon snack.

Upon their return, Pooh, Piglet, and Rabbit saw a strange sight.
"My, my," said Piglet. "Where did these colors come from?"
"It would appear," said Rabbit, "that *someone* has trespassed on our stage! Someone with purple paint, orange paint… and green paint!"
"But who?" puzzled Piglet. "This is certainly a mystery."

"And mysteries call for Super Sleuths!" announced Pooh.
"I'll go sound the alarm!"

Pooh sounded the Super Siren…

SSSuuunnndddPppperrr ssllIEEUUtthhs!

… and raised the Finder Flag!

The Super Sleuths—Darby, Tigger, Pooh, and Buster, too—all met in front of the Changing Tree.

"It looks like there's a mystery at the new theater," said Darby.

"That so?" asked Tigger. "I thought *The Busy Buzzy Bees* was a comedy."

"I mean," said Darby, "that the Finder Flag has a picture of the stage on it."

"Yes," piped up Pooh. "The theater has a rather mysterious guest— a colorful one, I might add."

"Come on, then," proclaimed Darby. "Let's go solve this mystery!"

"Any time, any place,
The Super Sleuths are on the case!"

"We left for a snack…" started Piglet.

"And when we came back…" added Pooh.

"We saw all these tracks!" said Rabbit. "We only had yellow, blue, and red paint."

"And now there are green, purple, and orange tracks on the stage," said Darby.

"This gives me stage fright!" said Piglet, shivering.

"Think, think, think!" said Darby. "Who else would have paint in the Hundred-Acre Wood? And how did the colors get onto the stage?"

"Yap, yap, yap!" barked Buster.

"What is it, Buster?" said Darby. "Are you paw-painting?"

"Hoo-hoo!" cried Tigger. "New paint tracks!"

"But those are Buster's tracks," said Piglet. "So… Buster must be the mystery painter."

"Let me look into this more closely…" said Tigger. "Aha! It appears that Buster has two-stepped into blue and waltzed into yellow—and made some very nice green puppy pawprints! You've got talent, Buster boy!"

"That's it!" said Darby! "When you mix blue and yellow, it makes green!"

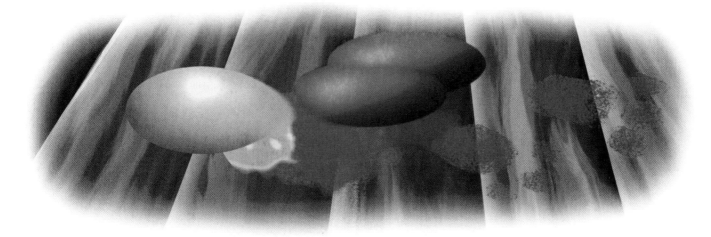

"I do believe," said Pooh, "that Buster is not the only one with green feet. Oh, bother."

"Silly ol' bear," said Darby. "You must have walked in blue and yellow paint—and made these big green tracks."

"Oh, my, oh, my, oh, my..." sighed Rabbit.

"Mine, too," nodded Piglet.

Darby smiled. "So, *you* two have stepped in paint! Let's see... what two colors make purple? And what makes orange? Let's find out!"

"Look!" said Piglet. "When red and yellow mix, they make orange. I must have stepped in both colors and made those orange tracks."

"A tiggerific color, I might add," added Tigger.

"Well, well," said Rabbit, "I must have stepped in red and blue— because they make purple."

"Mystery solved!" announced Tigger.

"And look at this," said Darby. "When all three mix together, they make brown! Hmmm... this gives me an idea…"

All the friends worked together. With only three cans of paint, they made enough colors to create the perfect backdrop for…

...one funny, honeyful comedy.
And another mystery was history.